Sharing is
CARING

Learning
to not be SELFISH

Jasmine Brooke

FOX EYE
PUBLISHING

Turtle found it difficult to **SHARE**. She liked to **KEEP** things for herself.

Turtle didn't like **SHARING** her toys.

She never wanted to **SHARE** her books.

When Turtle didn't **SHARE**, it often upset others, and that could be a problem.

3

4

On Monday, Mrs Tree took the class to the museum. She told everyone there were only a few books. She asked them all to form a pair so they could **SHARE**.

Monkey shared with Hippo. Lion shared with Gorilla. Parrot shared with Rhino. "Let's share too!" Giraffe said to Turtle.

Giraffe looked at Turtle's book. "No!" scowled Turtle. "It's **MINE**! I won't **SHARE**!"

Turtle held the book tightly, and she wouldn't let go.

That was **SELFISH**. It really wasn't **FAIR**. Turtle should have **SHARED**.

When they looked at the statues, Mrs Tree said everyone could take a photo. Mrs Tree said to **TAKE TURNS** with the camera.

Monkey was first. Next was Lion. Then Turtle took her turn. "My go!" smiled Gorilla. But Turtle held on to the camera. She wouldn't let go.

That was SELFISH.
It really wasn't FAIR.
Turtle should have
SHARED.

At the café, everyone looked for a table. Everyone looked for a seat. But there were not enough places. There was nowhere for Giraffe to sit.

Turtle had taken two seats. One for herself, another for her bag. She could see Giraffe needed a seat.

But Turtle didn't **CARE**.
That really wasn't **FAIR**.
Turtle should have **SHARED**.

"Sit with me," Monkey told Giraffe. "Let's **SHARE**."

"You're **SELFISH**," Giraffe told Turtle. But Turtle still didn't **CARE**.

Back at school, Mrs Tree thought it was time for a lesson. A lesson in how to **SHARE**. "Write about your day," she told the class. **"SHARE** your stories. Work as a pair."

Monkey chose Giraffe. Lion and Parrot made a pair. Rhino and Gorilla worked together.

But no one chose Turtle,
because she didn't like
to **SHARE**.

Working all **ALONE**, Turtle wished she was in a pair. She wished she could **SHARE**.

16

"Do you want to pair with me?" Mrs Tree asked kindly. "We could **SHARE** the work."

Now Turtle could see she had been **SELFISH**. She knew she hadn't been **FAIR**. "Yes, please," whispered Turtle, and she finally learnt to share!

Words and feelings

In this story, Turtle did not like sharing. She could be selfish and that upset others.

SHARE

KEEP

18

There are a lot of words to do with sharing and being selfish in this book. Can you remember all of them?

SELFISH

FAIR

CARE

Let's talk about behaviour

This series helps children to understand and manage difficult emotions and behaviours. The animal characters in the series have been created to show human behaviour that is often seen in young children, and which they may find difficult to manage.

Sharing is Caring

The story in this book examines issues around being selfish and not wanting to share. It looks at how being selfish and refusing to share can upset others.

   The book is designed to show young children how they can manage their behaviour and learn to share.

How to use this book

You can read this book with one child or a group of children. The book can be used to begin a discussion around complex behaviour such as learning to share.

   The book is also a reading aid, with enlarged and repeated words to help children to develop their reading skills.

How to read the story

Before beginning the story, ensure that the children you are reading to are relaxed and focused.

Take time to look at the enlarged words and the illustrations, and discuss what this book might be about before reading the story.

New words can be tricky for young children to approach. Sounding them out first, slowly and repeatedly, can help children to learn the words and become familiar with them.

How to discuss the story

When you have finished reading the story, use these questions and discussion points to examine the theme of the story with children and explore the emotions and behaviours within it:

- What do you think the story was about? Have you been in a situation in which you didn't want to share? What was that situation? For example, did you refuse to share a toy? Encourage the children to talk about their experiences.
- Talk about ways that people can cope with being selfish and not wanting to share. For example, think about how you would feel if someone didn't share with you. Talk to the children about what tools they think might work for them and why.
- Discuss what it is like to cope with someone who is selfish. Explain that Turtle did not want to share with her friends in the story, and that caused trouble both for her and her friends.
- Talk about why it is important to learn to share. Discuss why learning not to be selfish improves relationships.

Titles in the series

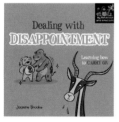 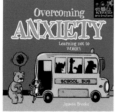  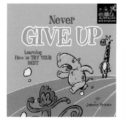 

  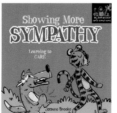  

First published in 2023 by Fox Eye Publishing
Unit 31, Vulcan House Business Centre,
Vulcan Road, Leicester, LE5 3EF
www.foxeyepublishing.com

Author: Jasmine Brooke
Art director: Paul Phillips
Cover designer: Emma Bailey & Salma Thadha
Editor: Jenny Rush

All illustrations by Novel

ISBN 978-1-80445-294-3

A catalogue record for this book is available from the
British Library

Printed in China